Ballerina!

by Peter Sís

Greenwillow Books *An Imprint of HarperCollinsPublishers*

Library of Congress Cataloging-in-Publication Data: Sís, Peter.   Ballerina! / by Peter Sís.   p.   cm.
"Greenwillow Books." Summary: A little girl puts on costumes of different colors and imagines herself
dancing on stage. ISBN 0-688-17944-4 (trade)   [1. Ballet dancing—Fiction. 2. Color—Fiction.] I. Title.
PZ7.S6219 Bal 2001 [E]—dc21 00-035401   First Edition   10 9 8 7 6

For my niece Tereza Sís

**Terry loves
ballet.**

She can't
wait to dance.

She puts on her tights
to warm up.

STRETCH

She puts on her
pink tutu and dances
The Nutcracker.

TWIRL

She puts on her
blue gown and dances
The Sleeping Beauty.

LEAP

**She puts on her
blue gown and dances
*The Sleeping Beauty.***

TWIRL

**She puts on her
red leotard and dances
a fire dance.**

TIPTOE

She puts on her
yellow turban and
dances a tiger dance.

REACH

**She puts on her
white feather boa and
dances *Swan Lake.***

DIP

She puts on her
green hat and dances
a spring dance.

FLUTTER

She puts on her
violet cape and
dances *Cinderella*.

F L O A T

She puts on her green, blue, violet, red, pink, yellow, and white scarves—

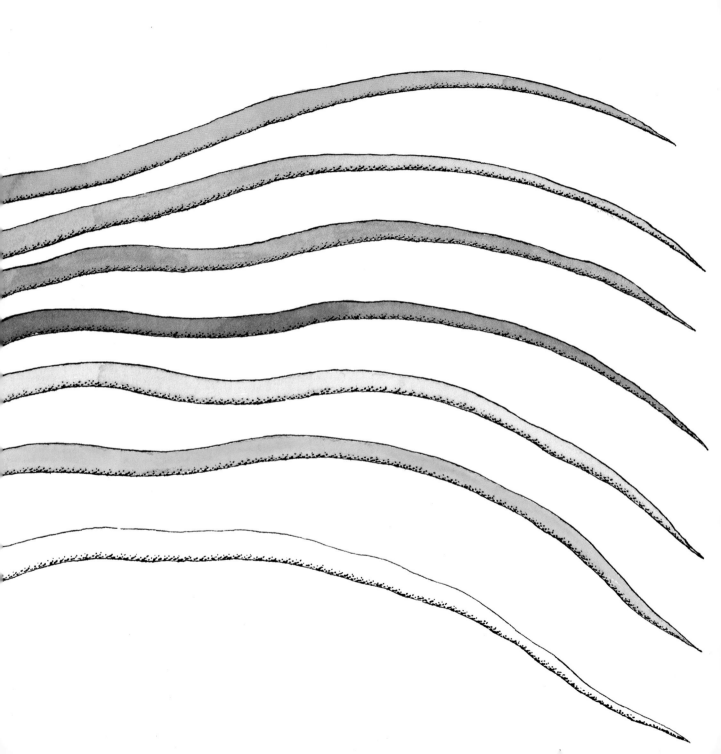

Her audience
claps and claps
and claps.

Her audience
claps and claps
and claps.

and is the best ballerina of all.